MADHUR RAJ

Kanjari

BLUEROSE PUBLISHERS
India | U.K.

Copyright © Madhur Raj 2024

All rights reserved by author. No part of this publication may be reproduced, stored in a retrieval system or transmitted in any form or by any means, electronic, mechanical, photocopying, recording or otherwise, without the prior permission of the author. Although every precaution has been taken to verify the accuracy of the information contained herein, the publisher assumes no responsibility for any errors or omissions. No liability is assumed for damages that may result from the use of information contained within.

BlueRose Publishers takes no responsibility for any damages, losses, or liabilities that may arise from the use or misuse of the information, products, or services provided in this publication.

For permissions requests or inquiries regarding this publication, please contact:

BLUEROSE PUBLISHERS
www.BlueRoseONE.com
info@bluerosepublishers.com
+91 8882 898 898
+4407342408967

ISBN: 978-93-6452-016-4

Cover design: Sadhana
Typesetting: Namrata Saini

First Edition: August 2024

About the Author

Madhur Raj is a Delhi bread lady. She is passed from Mudra Institute of Communication, Ahmedabad. Did Masters in Sociology from Delhi School of Economics. After a long career in Advertising she now writes. She writes film scripts and poetries too. She writes in Hindi and English both. She takes inspiration from real struggle and her late father Dr Devakar. She is passionate about writing. She had started writing in college only.

'Kanjiri come fast, blood sugar level is going down'. Kanjiri hears her mother's call and rushes downstairs towards her parent's room, where her mother was doing her father's dialysis. Kanjiri was about to enter the room that she hears another shout 'get some sugar fast'. Kanjiri changes her direction to the kitchen. Papa's sugar levels have dipped before also but mother had never panicked like this! Is anything serious today?

Thinking aloud she rushes to her parent's room with sugar in a bowl.

Parent's room was looking like a mini hospital room. On one side of the bed, blood pressure instrument was laying ideal, medicine strips were scattered and various bandages and gauges were the decorations. Near the bed was standing a long steel apparatus kind of thing. A poly bag containing yellow liquid was hanging over it and through a tube that yellow thing was going into the father's stomach.

Man, this sight had always troubled Kanjiri. Though mother had asked her help many times, she had purposely stayed away. She could not see this mutilation. And her mother thought she does not want to take responsibility.

'Kanjiri what are you thinking, I can't understand what he is saying'. Mom's words brought Kanjiri back from her thoughts and she attentively leaned towards her father. He was mumbling. She tried hearing, as mother's ears were no longer strong enough to hear faint voices. 'He is saying he needs glucose', he is suggesting we take him to hospital',

Kanjiri informs her mother. Mother panics, 'now? at night? how will we go?'.

'don't worry I will call Saran we will handle', Kanijiri assures her.

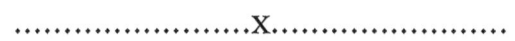

Kanjiri was sitting on a bench in a semi private hospital. Her mother was sleeping next to her in a sitting posture, her head resting on Kanjiri's shoulder. Kanjiri also wanted to sleep but she was not able to. When she had asked doctor about taking her father back in the morning, he had not answered very clearly. He just said, 'we will see'. Was there anything serious? He just needed glucose! Doctor's indecisive answer was troubling Kanjiri and had taken her sleep away. She purposely had not told mother about this and smiled seeing her sleeping, like a log.

Kanjari had already informed Kapil, her younger brother, about father's hospitalisation. He had arranged the money and now she was relaxed.

'Kapil and Kanjiri'– her parents were so fond of their children's rhythmic names, whereas for Kapil, at times this was a source of embarrassment.

His friends used to tease him saying, 'his parents are believer of 'K' factor, much practiced in Bollywood'. Infact one day after coming from college he had really asked mother, if it this was true and father had said 'yes', just to tease him.

How time has changed, Kapil is now a well placed software engineer in Singapore. His fun loving and money making philosophy has gone under major change. He is not only evolved himself materially but also spiritually. He is now a third level practitioner of advanced meditation and a devotee of Shiv. Papa had started saying, 'he is my Kapil muni'.

In college Kapil was a very un- decisive youth and kanjiri was his self acclaimed teacher in explaining life's philosophical issues. But roles seem to have reversed now. Today Kanjiri is much greateful to Kapil for solving her life entanglements.

From breaking up with Siddharth to various professional and personal upheavals, Kapil had stood by her all along, even to the extent of making parents understand Kanjiri's point of view. Kapil always fondly said, 'I am paying you for the petrol money which you used to lend me for my scooter while going on my dates'. That time Kanjiri used to work for an ad agency and it was a boon for Kapil. Actually Kapil always admired Kanjiri's mental faculties and resolute attitude towards life's difficulties. And so did his parents.

The day Kapil's marriage was decided, was a day of mixed feelings for his parents. The joy of their son's marriage was not complete – their elder daughter was yet unmarried and had also announced the decision of

'not marrying'. Kapil had asked Kanjiri to get married before his marriage but she had softly declined. After Siddharth, men had become a non- issue in her life.

Kapil's marriage had given a new lease of life in kanjiri parent's small world.

She had taken all the work in her hand as Kapil could not take off from work for long. But the main reason was her own guilt of not being able to give that pleasure to her parents. Kanjiri's last job had ended with a broil with the creative director and she had thrown herself in the marriage work completely.

Kanjiri was well versed with her father's literary prowess and she was determined to make use of that in Kapil's marriage. It had taken full one day for her to cajole her father to write Kapil's 'sehara*' for the shadi.

She finally fixed a drink for her father in the evening and he wrote beautiful lines in 15 minutes flat-

"subhya ki kaliyo se banaya hai, yeh sahera

os ki bondo se saja hai, yeh sehara

kalpana our prabhat ke armaan ka hai, yeh sahera

kanjiri ke gunjar se sawara hai, yeh sahera

kapil aur bindia ke pyar ka hai, yeh sahara

aap ki duao ka talabdar hai, yeh sahara".

Bindia bhabhi's father had liked these lines so much that he was going on saying 'Mr. Srivastav once more...once more'. Though many people had done Shero-Shayairi in Kapil's marriage but 'Sahera' became the show-stopper and it brought big smile on papa's face.

But this happiness could not stay for too long as papa was soon diagnosed with kidney failure and was put on dialysis within one year of Kapil's marriage. Mom was devastated.

If Sahil bhaiya had not visited from US that year it would have been very difficult for Kanjiri to contain mom.

Sahil was the son of papa's elder brother. He was another pillar in Kanjiri's life. Since he could not attend Kapil's marriage he thought it incumbent to visit us, hearing papa's condition. This had given Kapil also a much needed respite, as he was saved from taking off from work.

Sahil bhaiya's doctor friend in AIIMS was much appreciated help in that testing time. He had done all leg work, from fixing appointments with Nephrologists at Medwin Hospital to papa's counseling. Papa had become a child in that phase and was adamantly refusing to go under operation for dialysis. But Sahil bhaiya's friend was a seasoned doctor and bhaiya himself was also someone to reckon with. For Kajiri, Sahil was a fatherly figure, though their relations had become little strained when Kanjiri refused one of the marriage proposal, which he had got for her. That was the time she was going around with Sidharth.

How much she wished now that she had accepted that proposal. But what had to happen, had happened.

....

Sahera – is the name of the headgear (decoration) which bridegroom wears in Indian marriage. In north Indian marriages there is a full ceremony in which everyone says somethings in appreciation of that gear.

....

She glances at her watch, it was 5 a.m. She carefully places mom's head on the backside of the bench and lifts her jammed legs to action – 'she must go and talk to the doctor, its morning now'. Kanjiri enters Dr. Vinay's cabin and was surprised to see him working.

Her 'goodmorning' was well greeted but still there was something thoughtful about him. 'How is papa doctor sahib, can we take him now?' Dr. Vinay, 'well I need to talk to you Kanjiri, would you like some coffee'? 'No sir, you tell me honestly what you have to say, trust me I can take it', Kanjiri assured him. 'ya ya I have seen you throughout, and have to tell 'you only' because you are alone taking care of your parents here. Well Kanjiri your dad has developed a severe infection and because of that he has high fever'.

Kanjiri– infection? How did that happen?

Doctor- well sometimes it happens in water dialysis patients.

'But we had changed blood dialysis to this one because you had said it was easy and better', Kanjiri said almost blamingly.

Doctor- see dialysis patients are susceptible to infections, be it water or blood dialysis, as they are exposed to foreign element. Don't worry we would be treating him. But before starting the medicine I had to tell you.

Dr. Vinay was head of the Nephrology department and Kanjiri had no reason to doubt his diagnosis but still she was feeling cheated. She reluctantly gave her consent and left the room with heaviness in her heart.

In her bemused state she turned to ICU as her father was transferred to ICU now. Since she was carrying a little note from the doctor she was given an easy access to the usual cordoned off area. Though her father was comfortably sleeping, all surrounding techno-medical equipment was creating a very eerie feeling. Kanjiri made the brave effort to contain herself in the room and asked the attending nurse for all the details. His father's fever had not come down with normal fever medicines. In the morning only Dr. Vinay had decided to give him a strong anti-biotic injection. Nurse was waiting for the doctor now. Kanjiri brushed her hand on her father's forehead and quickly left the room.

Kanjiri gets up suddenly calling 'papa...'. She was woken up from a very real looking dream and finds herself in the private ward room of Medwin hospital. It was 4 a.m in the morning and mom was asleep next to her. She had seen such dreams before also..like someone telling her to do something. This time in her dream her father was lying upside-down surrounded by her mother and grandparents (now dead) and her father turns back the moment she applies 'Bhabhut*' on his forehead.

Was this dream telling her to do something? She gets up and locates her mom's purse which always has some

Bhabhut in it and walks out of the room with the Bhabhut packet in her hand. She reaches in front of the ICU unit but the guard stops her from entering. She very humbly shows the Bhabhut packet, also tells him about her dream to the guard man and requests him to go and apply

*Bhabhut on her father's forehead.

....

*Bhabhut – kind of religious ash.

Guard becomes moved by the request and allows Kanjiri to go inside herself and apply it on her father's forehead.

Kanjari is standing in front of her father's bed. Father was sitting on the bed, in almost dazed situation. Kanjari goes near him and puts Bhabhut on his forehead. He mumbles. Kanjari takes her ear near him and asks what happened. He says," here they are not doing anything. Take me from here." Kanjari understands that he wants to go to another hospital. That very night Kapil comes. Kanjari had already told her mother that her father wanting to go to another hospital. All decide to take him to Apollo Hospital. One of the relative was doctor at Apollo and he helped Kanjari's father a lot before also. He was a general physician. He diagnosed that Kanjari's father had problem in the stomach. In 15 days Kanjari's father recovered and came back to home.

Doctor had advised him blood dialysis twice a week. So Kanjari and her mother's life revolved around her father's medication. Slowly life was coming to normal. The emergency had passed. Sahil bhaia still calls once a week to inquire about Kanjari's father for which she and her mom are quiet grateful.

Night has fallen. Mummy and papa have retired to their room. Kanjari is in the balcony listening to Phill Collins over the head phones. She loves Phill Collin's Susodio number. It's a peppy number and has put Kanjari in a much peaceful state. Kanjari is pondering on recent events, as to, how papa has got next life after being shifted to Apollo? It really was a miracle that papa got well as his condition after infection was quiet bad. Silently Kanjari thanked god for this and went to sleep.

Kanjari wakes feeling quiet serious and goes to drawing room where mom and papa are having morning tea. Mom says 'kanjari good morning'.

Kanjari replies back 'good morning mom'. Mom, "Kanjari take tea from the kettle. It is still hot". Kanjari "acha mummy"". Kanjari is sipping tea looking out of window looking over the lawn. Kanjari always takes much time to uncoil in mornings. But today she was in quiet serious mood.

Reason was the dream she saw early morning. Much real looking dream was a haze where a female voice is calling out Kanjari "

kajari...kanjari..wake up to your real life..become aware of your inner self".

Suddenly the hazy smoke gives way to a picture of goddess Saraswati.

Who much to Kanjari's surprise was speaking in English but had Veena in her hand. Voice further tells Kanjari - " start taking your writing talent seriously, play with words and win the world'. Kanjari is looking out of window and pondering, 'what kind of dream it was'. It's true that she loves writing but never took it very seriously. She remembers her days of Delhi School of Economics, where she had written a seminar titled- "Changing Face of Money'. It was much appreciated by Prof. Veena Das. Suddenly she feels a strong urge to read her old poems. She takes out her much loved dairy in which she has hidden her golden words. She opens pages of her first poem –

That's It

I pass the day......hoping it will

reveal something new.

Though mundane becomes the reality,

I surprise myself with my " improved facade".

Passing through the undulated plains of my thoughts,

Sometimes I create ripples, only

to end my day.....

Searching for some smoldering

flakes in the ash heap...

I dig every evening ...just to add

more to my treasured Waste !.

This poem reminds Kanjari of her D School days. Those days were spent reading Marx, Weber, Ayn Rand and to top it all Sartre's existentialism.

Life now seems to have taken a full circle from idealism to reality of, earning a living. Suddenly mummy calls her loudly and Kanjari wakes up from her literary muse.

Mother - Kanjari, " what are you day dreaming about" ?

Kanjari- oh mummy, I was reading my some old poems. I just felt like.

Mother – ok. You read I am going to kitchen.

Kanjari is still overlooking the garden and pondering over some stark life issues, as to where her life is taking?

What should she do to make her life more fruitful?.

Papa calls for Kanjari. Papa – Kanjari . Kanjari- Ha papa. Papa – kanjari, show us some movie today, some good one. You know so many. Kanjari walks to her father. Kanjari- papa, let me show you a very nice movie of Dharmendra. Papa- which one, I have seen many movies of Dharmendra.

Kanjari- I am sure, you have not seen this movie. Its name is Dillagi. It's a romantic drama of Dharmendra and Hema Malini. I have seen it, I want to show to you.

Papa – ok, put it and tell your mummy also to come.

All three are watching the movie. Papa- oh! its Basu Chaterjee movie. Must be good. Kanjari- ya. In whole movie papa and mummy are laughing and Kanjari is in her thoughts. By seeing this movie she gets some inspiration. She comes up with a plot of a romantic comedy set in different tone.

Kanjari goes to her table in the room and takes out the laptop and starts writing. She starts a romantic comedy, which after five pages takes shape of a hindi movie script. This story's tone is different and Kanjari is surprised that she is writing after a long time and that too a hindi movie. Papa and mummy also ask her what she is writing but she says she will tell when its finished.

................x.................

After a week her movie finishes and she tells everyone on the breakfast table that she has written a movie script. Both mummy and papa are surprised. She learns over the week, that papa has told Sahil bhaia and Kapil also. Both send her whats up and congratulate. Infact, Sahil says, 'Kanjari you were destined to write'. I have read your poetries." But midst this conversation she feels that people are not so happy as she had expected. House people are more surprised than happy. Kapil also did not congratulate her, 'just said, good to hear, you are doing something'.

Apart from the big movie, Kanjari also writes some short scripts. To market her film she attends some short film festivals and meet many small time film makers. But she does not get success in getting her film made. She also tells Kapil to help but not much of success. In the festival some participants tell her that Bollywood is a jungle and many established filmmakers lift newcomer's scripts and deny them all credit. This makes Kanjari very depressed and she feels her movie will never see the day light. Two years have passed Kanjari's struggle is on.

Kanjari is called for a poetry festival whose name is Pinrest Festival. People are asked to present their writing creations on

theme of 'Bollywood'. Kanjari dresses up after a long time. Mummy says ' good to see you all dreassed up,

where are you going?'. Kanjari," I am going for a poetry festival". Mummy – oh that's nice. Kanjari reaches Trivoli gardens, Chaterpur, where festival is organized. Whole place is bannered with the Pinrest Festival visuals, so she finds no problem in finding the place. She registers her name in the participant's list and takes a front seat. Festival is inaugurated and chief guest is Javed Akhtar who is noted Shayer in Bollywood. He says few lines to the participants.

Javed Akhtar- Aaj ka din kafi naya sa hai. Jaha logo ko Bollywood theme pe poetry kahene ke liye kaha gaya hai.

Mai paheli bar aisa koi festival dekh raha hu. Pinrest organisers ko mai badhai deta hu, Bollywood ko itni bari hasti samajhne ke liye...jo woh hai.

Sabhi Bollywood ke gano per thumka laga lete hai per poetry kahna ka andaz kafi nirala hai. Bollywood ke logo ki jindagi kafi serious business hai kyoki kafi struggle hai is line me. So Best of luck everyone. Thanks.

The moment Javed Ahtar speech finishes one man rushes and sits next to her. He is in quiet disheveled state. He says – Hi, I am Mayur. Guess

Javed Akhtar's speech I missed. Kanjari says nothing, only looks at him.

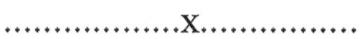

Many participants have said their poem. Kanjari is hearing carefully. Her name is announced. She gets up hurriedly and goes to the stage.

Kanjari – thanks for giving me opportunity to express her creation on Bollywood. Kanjari,"my first poem is explaining how a new entrant enters

Bollywood". She narrates: This poems name is "Chala chukander mukkadar banane".

Chala chukander mukkadar banane

Sach pe phisla,gam me nikhara Seekha duniya ka khel

Lagai bazi armano ki Sajai dukaan samjhote ki Chadayi parvan dileri ki Kholi pol kamane ki

Jeeti dimag ki dil pe jung-2 Charaha sunhara chashma Aur phir dekha duniya ka rung Chala Chukander mukkadar banane Chala Chukander mukkadar banana People clap. Audience - very nice, very nice. Kanjari -'my next poem is "Identity Crisis".

Identity crisis!

Jo aajkal sharukh khan ko bhi ho rahi hai.

Jab filmi hero heroin ko identity crisis hone lagti hai To woh apne ko, naye AVTAR me launch karne lagte hai jaise Ritik roshan ne apne ko launch kiya KRISH ke roop me Tare Jami me Aamir dikhe RANCHODAS ke roop me Aur Sharukh ji ne to, Ra-One me, RAVAN ke naam ko ek nayi spelling hi de dali.

Aap ko pata hai, marketing language me, is technique ko kya kahate hai – "apne ko time ke saath REINVENT karna".

Aur is khel me sabse aage hai apne Big B Bachan sahab is umar me bhi, har 2-3 saal me, ek reinvented role me dikhte hai Unka Zanjir se karorepati tak ka safar, pata nahi unko kitne naye janm de chuka hai Hamare bhagvan ko bhi unse seekhna chahiye...reinventing ki takneek Bhaiya admi ke pas jo masterpiece hai - called 'DIMAG' (Points towards his head) Woh aane wale samay me, pata nahi kya kya technology invent karega, allah hi jane Hum to shayad na ho, Lekin ane wali nasle, jarror witness karengi, Human race ka woh mukam.

....

Kanjari, " that's it". Hope you people liked it. Thanks.

Audience - liked it very much. Clapping.

Midst clapping Kanjari comes and sits on her chair. Mayur congratulates her. She smiles. Whole program goes on for an hour. It was interesting. They announce that now one can proceed towards Tea.

Kanjari is standing in a corner sipping Tea. Mayur comes and joins her. Mayur, " hello, your poems were really nice. Great sense of humor".

Kanjari, 'thanks". Mayur – "do you write regulary". Kanjari – not regulary. These were written quiet some time back. I am great fan of Bollywood". Mayur- "ya that I am seeing". Kanjari laughs. Mayur –'what else do you write'. Kanjari-" well I have written a Bollywood movie".

Mayur – really!

So are you coming for tomorrow for the film screening. Kanjari- ya, I am coming. One of my short film is getting screened. Mayur – oh that's nice. So lets meet tomorrow. Both move out of the building. It takes one hour to reach home. Chatterpur is quiet far. Its late in the evening.

Kanjari straight goes to the dinning table, eats dinner and sleeps. Next day again is a busy start. Mummy says, "she has no time to talk". Kanjari smiles and leaves for the Pinerest festival'.

Kanjari sits at the usual seat. Screening is about to start. First film is her's only. Mayur again is late today. He rushes and sits next to her. Both exchange greetings and start watching the film. Organiser

announces Kanjari's short film Tamashbeen. Tamashbeen is sort of satire on high flying society, shot in the background of Bollywood.

Audience really likes the character of Sharad Maskara who is a journalist and film finishes midst clapping. There were three films to be shown, all finish, Mayur turns to Kanjari and congratulates her.

Kanjari is having dinner with some participants and Mayur. As dinner finishes Mayur says to Kanjari that he wants to talk to her. They go to the Coffee Shop of Trivoli Gardens and sit on one table.

..............x............

Kanjari- Yes Mayur what you want to talk about. Mayur- Kanjari, I am impressed by your writing skills. Tell me more about the feature film which you have written. I am interested in producing it, if its good. Kanjari – It's a romantic drama movie. Mayur – Can you show me the script. Kanjari- well, I can show some pages but just now I don't have anything. Mayur – Ok then let's meet next Sunday, as I am busy in a shoot for week. Kanjari says – ok. That night Kanjari sleeps late. She is thinking about Mayur and is apprehensive of the coming meeting.

Mayur calls Kanjari twice over the weekend. It becomes quiet clear to Kanjari that Mayur wants to be in touch with her. She is little surprised that Mayur is showing so much of interest in her. Finally Sunday comes and Kanjari tells papa and mummy that she is going to meet a film producer. Papa eyes her little sheepishly as he senses something more. Mayur and Kanjari meet in C.P in Delhi in restaurant "The Connaught".

Mayur as usual comes little late. He is little relaxed like all creative people, while Kanjari because of training in Client handling is quiet professional in dealings. Kanjari gives four pages of the movie script to Mayur to read. He reads it attentively and praises the writing skill. Slowly he turns the conversation quiet personal as he asks her," why she is not married till now". She admits she had an affair which did not work out. He also tells her about his flings and admits that he has not been serious till now but as he is already 35yrs now he is thinking about marriage. In the same sentence he surprises Kanjari by asking her hand in marriage. Kanjari gets little flustered being asked for the marriage. Mayur smiles on her discomfort and holds her hand. She takes away her hand and tells Mayur to tell about himself. Mayur discloses that he has noone. He was raised by his grandfather as his parents died in an accident long back. But now his grandfather is also nomore. She shows regret on this news and assures him that she will let him know about the marriage offer. Kanjari also wants to settle in life but with a person who will have compatibility with her.

Kanjari and Mayur get married same year in the start of winters. Kanjari agrees Mayur to stay with her parents only as no one is there in Mayur house. Both go to honeymoon in Ooty. They come refreshed and start on their movie project. Mayur reads Kanjari's movie script. Kanjari is preparing the movie synopsis to be sent to various producers.

In the middle Kanjari's mother gets hospitalized because of her weak heart. Kanjari's responsibility at home also grow but she is trying her best. Slowly Mayur and Kanjari realise that their project is not moving ahead as no one is coming forward to invest money in their movie. Some say the movie script is very maturely written and they want some different kind of romance in the script. So Kanjari refuses such kind of producers who don't want culturally strong movie.

Mayur explains to Kanjari that people in Bollywood are very old fashioned regarding women and Kanjari is quiet an astute negotiator which many can't take. Kanjari has started giving up but Mayur does not give up and keeps looking for a producer and director.

But Kanjari and Mayur start drawing apart due to frustration. Finally they separate their ways and Mayur moves to Mumbai. Again Kanjari fall backs on her parents.

...............x...................

Mayur does not tell his plans to Kanjari. Kanjari thinks that Mayur was just an opportunist but reality was different. Mayur really likes Kanjari and is ready to do anything for her.

He does not tell Kanjari that it's a game of 'destiny' which people are playing with her. No one wants to give her destiny. Kanjari does not know that many in Bollywood know about her script as its written quiet brilliantly. Producers are not agreeing as many established actors are not agreeing to act in her movie. As they want to take Kanjari's destiny. Finally Mayur approaches 'Maya', who is an established heroin in the Bollywood.

He tells her to act in the movie and also help find a producer. Maya shows different kind of interest in Mayur and takes him to her bed. Mayur plays along as he wants Kanjari to succeed and knows what Kanjari's movie mean to her. Mayur stays with Maya for an year as she is alone. Mayur enters into a deal with Maya, that he will stay for an year with Maya and in return she will do Kanjiri's movie. One year passes and Mayur is excited about meeting Kanjari. Many times he thinks of ringing Kanjari but refrains as he still does not have anything for Kanjari.

..................x..................

After sleeping with Maya, Mayur goes back home and cries. He accepts this sacrifice in the way of making Kanjari's movie. He still likes Kanjari and wants to help her and himself. He is sure that he will meet Kanjari when he has some solid contract for her.

Currently he gets some small production jobs from Maya and is somehow managing his livelihood. This way one year has passed, he wonders how Kanjari is doing. He is still dependent on Maya and wants Kanjari's contract so that he can also be independent. One day he directly confronts Maya and asks, " will she work in Kanjari's movie". She laughs and says- 'you have still not forgotten her', OK I will work. Maya is a very good-looking woman but very competitive. She finally agrees that she will behave well with Kanjari, as she is jealous of her.

After getting confirmation from Maya, Mayur decides to go back to Kanjari. He knows that with Kanjari he will make money. Mayur wants to keep both women, one for bed and one for money. Kanjari is not aware of this nature of Mayur. Mayur boards the plane and surprises Kanjari and her parents at Delhi. Kanjari cries seeing him but regains her composer. She was meeting Mayur after a longtime. Mom is giving Tea to Mayur. Papa calls Kanjari to the library and expresses his apprehensions about Mayur. But Kanjari is so happy that she registers nothing what her father is saying. She just says to her father- " don't worry, nothing will happen".

And rushes back to the drawing room, where Mayur is sitting.

Mayur takes out some gifts for Papa and Mummy. Then Kanjari and Mayur move to their room. Kanjari complains that he has got nothing for her. Mayur says, he has got Vada Pao for her from Mumbai and both laugh. Then he tells Kanjari to close her eyes. Mayur opens his suitcase and takes out a sari and drapes over her shoulders.

Kanjari opens her eyes and is delighted to see a Chiffon designer sari. Kanjari quickly goes to bathroom and wears that sari. She is looking nice and Mayur embraces her, both mingle in love.

Kanjari

Over the evening tea when Kanjari is pouring tea for everyone, Mayur announces that he has an important news for Kanjari.

Kanjari gets excited. Mayur takes out a letter from his pocket and gives it to her. She reads it expectantly. Mom also asks- 'what is it'. Father is quietly sipping his tea. He is just watching everything. Kanjari tells everybody – 'it's a letter from Kapoor producers, saying that – "they are interested to make my movie with famous actress Maya in it". Mom congratulates, Papa just reads the letter and says nothing.

....................x....................

Next day Kanjari calls Kapil and gives the news that Mayur is back and tells him about the letter too. Kapils tells her that he already knows as Papa has already called him. Kanjari wonders what all Papa has told Kapil, as he is not so happy with Mayur's comeback.

Kanjari has dressed up quiet professionally in pant and tops, as she is going to meet Kapoor Producers along with Mayur. Meeting is set in Surya Sofetel at New Friends Colony. Producer sees full film script and Kanjari tells him to hire Imran Khureshi as Director. All this was arranged by Maya and Kanjari has much to thank her. After a week, Imran Khureshi arrives and meeting is at the same place, Surya Sofetel.

Imran was an enigmatic personality and it does not take much time for Kanjari to develop an awe for him.

She could not believe she is sitting with Imarn Khureshi. Further meetings were done at Kanjari's place only. It takes one month to discuss full script, songs and location etc. Imran tells them that it will take 3 months now to get songs prepared, hire actors and designers etc. Mayur and Kanjari head for Kasauli hill station to unwind and enjoy. All is well between them. Mom is much happy, papa is also accepting the situation slowly.

Days are passing in shooting the film. Kanjari goes daily at the location and rehearsals. Mayur is taking care of production. One day after seeing shooting of a funny scene, Kanjari comes into a very good mood. She gets up to look for Mayur on the sets. She heads toward make up rooms.

She finds him in Maya's makeup room. She is shocked to see them in an embrace. She can't move. Then only Maya says something and Kanjari hides behind a wall. They don't see her.

Kanjari is quietly sitting next to Mayur in the car while going back home. For Kanjari life has come to an end. Few days pass in numbness. Mayur asks her –'whats the matter" but she does not say anything. Kanjari has stopped talking to Mayur. Kanjari has become totally incommunicado. She keeps quiet at film shooting too. One day Mayur confronts her and asks – "whats the matter?" Kanjari is all bottled up and tells him that she saw him and Maya together in the makeup room. Mayur has no answer. Kanjari is crying and is not able to contain her sorrow.

Mayur is explaining her that all that is part and parcel of gaining success. He needed Maya's help and thus he is doing her sexual favors. But Kanjari is too much in pain and shocked state to listen to him. She tells Mayur to leave and film stops.

....................x...................

Days have stopped for Kanjari. She does not know what to do. Her only activity is to share Whatsapp messages with Kapil and Sahil. Kapil comes to meet her. He spends some days with her. He reassures that life is a circle of events, that's why it's called "Circle of Life". Life will surely take another turn for better and she will come out more enlightened. He gives mythological example from Indian history. Story of Sita, Draupadi, Ahilya and Rani Laxmi

Bai. All have been through great turmoil in their life and have been the cause of change in philosophies. Their power to fight and come out has been inspiration of many women. Modern women should take courage from their experiences. Kapil dialogues console her but Kanjari does not understand why Kapil is taking example of such big historical figures. Well, what she does not know, is that life has yet to show many turns to her, which Kapil knows. Kapil ends the dialogue by saying that Sahil wants to come to meet her in this downtime, she agrees.

Kanjari is expecting Sahil, as he has sent a mail that he will reach India this Sunday. Sahil is a jovial person but this time he looked quiet serious and touched Kanjari's shoulders with concern. After taking dinner all settle for bed. Sahil tells Kanjari that he will talk to her after breakfast in the morning. Kanjari till late night is wondering, what Sahil will talk with her. As Kanjari comes for breakfast, sees her father and Sahil talking but they stop, the moment they see her. After breakfast Sahil tells Kanjari to sit in the library room with him.

Sahil finds Kanjari very sad. He holds her hand and tells her that she can tell him everything. Kanjari releases her pent-up emotions and says she is heartbroken over Mayur. Sahil explains that Mayur had to do all that for profession. Many successful women are sexually demanding and Maya is such a one. It looks, Sahil had a talk with Mayur.

Sahil also says that a man is different from a woman fundamentally. It's difficult for a man to control himself sexually than for a woman. He almost talked like a doctor which he is. He also explains that Kanjari can't stop her film in anger. It's not professional.

He takes promise from her that she will forgive Mayur and tells her that he will call Mayur to Delhi.

Mayur comes and asks for forgiveness from Kanjari.

Kanjari's father is maintaining diplomatic silence. He is a scientist and has lot of patience. Kanjari accepts his plea as she also wants her movie to finish. She learns a major lesson in life i.e 'to take life, as it comes'.

On her decision, papa says- "this is the 'Salt and Pepper' aspect of life which everyone has to taste".

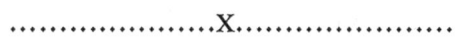

Film resumes, Kanjari is going everyday to keep her busy. Maya and Kanjari are not on talking terms.

Things are little tense at sets as everyone knows about the triangle of Kanjari, Mayur and Maya. One day Sahil arrives at sets, just to encourage Kanjari. After lunch Sahil does not come for a longtime after saying – 'he is going to bathroom'.

Kanjari goes to look for him. After seeing many rooms, she finds Sahil and Mayur in Maya's makeup room. They both seem to be in heated discussion.

This room probably has destiny to show reality to Kanjari.

From outside he hears Sahil's voice – "you must keep her in control. Before marriage only I had told you she has destiny to write films. She can do many things. She is the best mind in the world." Mayur – " I must tell her that everyone has her mind". Sahil-"don't tell her anything. I had told you before marriage only that you will have to contain her. How she got to know about Maya? She should have not known. Just keep her happy."

Kanjari is stunned.

She never knew that Sahil knew Mayur before marriage. What are they talking that 'I have best mind in the world'. How it is possible. What is happening in her life? Why everyone is appearing mysterious to her. She did not want to tell her parents anything. She had given them enough pain by marrying Mayur. Days are passing in tension. She is just keeping a façade in front of everyone. But one Sunday she is not able to contain herself and confronts Mayur.

Mayur gets scared when he hears that Kanjari has heard Sahil and Mayur's talks at the sets. He almost cries and holds Kanjari by shoulder. He admits that he has hidden things from her. He agrees to tell everything. Kanjari comes to know her life secret, that Sahil is world's biggest spiritual leader (Yogi). He has created a worldwide web of vibrations and everyone is connected to Kanjari's mind. Sahil calls Kanjari's mind the best in the world and world's much advancement is guided by Kanjari's mind. She does not understand, how it is possible? She also comes to know that people hail Sahil for giving them success by working through Kanjari's mind.

Things are beyond Kanjari's. She tells Mayur that she will ask Sahil about this, but he warns against it. He does'nt chalks a very good picture of Sahil. Kanjari is confused.

Kanjari is just spending time thinking about her life. She has started keeping quiet. Mayur also talks to her very less. On sets, he has openly started staying with Maya. Kanjari confronts Mayur about this, but he does not listen. He just tells her to accept the way things are. They exchange heated words. Next day Sahil comes. He had been staying with his friend with whom he was opening a medical center in Delhi.

Mom had called Sahil as she was much concerned about Kanjari and Mayur.

Sahil scolds Mayur and tells him to be considerate to Kanjari. He even agrees to tell her everything about her life. He tells her she has a big destiny. Her mind is sought after by everyone. Sahil is a member of a think-tank group, whose meetings are conducted in Switzerland. This group calls Kanjari's mind the supreme mind. In world many people have her vibrations and they are inventing big things by taking guidance from mind. Sahil further tells that he has created 'out of body' creatures from human soul matter. Something like 'ant-man'. These bodies are allotted to some intelligent minds and they study

Kanjari's mind. They have made many inventions. World has much to owe to Kanjari for it's development. Kanjari is stunned. Does not know what to say to Sahil. He reassures her that everything will be all right.

After this revelation she approaches her father and mother as she comes to know from Sahil that they all know about her mind and what Sahil is doing. Father tells his life history to her. He says when Kanjari was small they were very poor. He was just a small scientist, living on a meager salary. Unfortunately, academics does not bring material prosperity. He tells

Sahil who was studying medical in USA to do something. After he finishes his studies, he comes to India to meet him. He tells that with medicine he has also learnt Reiki and meditation. He tells, he has also learnt past life regression, which can absolve Karma of humankind. He tells this helps in health issues too as all this is due to Karma accumulation.

Kanjari father asks," can he do past life regression of Kanjari as she keeps very sick and gets severe cough every winter". He agrees and what he discovers, that Kanjari's mind is one of the best. He has done past life regression of so many people but has not found such a developed mind.

Sahil tells that he wants to tell everyone that Kanjari has best mind. He also finds a way to earn by giving Kanjari's vibration to people, through which they can do better work in life. This brings prosperity for Kanjari's parents too.

Kanjari's father reveals that he, mom, kapil and Sahil, all have taken Kanjari's vibration. Infact government also has taken her mind's vibration and lot of development in the world has happened through Kanjari's mind. Kanjari's mind is going in circles hearing all this. She feels good hearing that she has best mind but feels angry that her people never told her about this. So, this was Kanjari's life's story and she takes many days to digest it.

One day Mayur comes to Kanjari and says he urgently needs one crore. Now Kanjari is supporting her family. All are dependent on her, even Sahil. Sahil's medical practice had stopped because some friend cheated him. He has been staying on meagre money for long time. Kanjari asks Mayur, why he needs so much money, he does not say anything. Just tells her to give him money. She refuses as she is not very happy with him.

Days are passing.

As Sahil is staying with her things are fine. He keeps everyone in jovial mood. One day Kanjari, Sahil and Mayur are walking from a restaurant to home. Kanjari is behind them. She is walking and listening to music on the mobile. Suddenly a van arrives, stands next to Kanjari. Four men come out. One puts a cloth on her mouth, with chloroform in it. She tries to shout but could not. Sahil and Mayur are much ahead. She falls unconscious and knows nothing. Men put her in the van and take her.

After some time Sahil looks back to see why no voice is coming from behind.

He does not find Kanjari, Mayur also looks back. When both realise that Kanjari is not to be seen anywhere, they panic. They run to the house and tell Kanjari's parents that Kanjari is nowhere to be found. Sahil calls the police. Police comes and both Mayur and Sahil again go to search her but find nothing. Sadly they come back. No one sleeps that night.

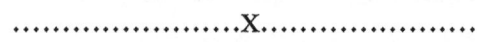

Its 7 in the morning. Kanjari wakes up with heavy head, discovers herself in a middle- class house. She runs in the room, then bangs on the door. After sometime someone opens the door.

Two men enter the room with one cup tea and some biscuits. They say that they won't do anything to her as they just want money i.e one crore. She is so panicked that she agrees to pay immediately without arguing. She has her card in the purse. She goes to bank with those two men. She goes to the bank manager and greets him.

She tells him, she has to withdraw 1 cr. Bank manager ask her,' if everything is ok, as she needs such a big amount immediately'. She says,' all is fine' but winks. Two men are standing behind her. She asks for paper and says I am writing my account number. With the number she also writes – "keep your CC tv on and take today's footage". Two men do not realise anything. Two men take the money in suitcase and all three leave the bank. They leave her in front of her house.

She runs inside the house. All come running to her. Mom and papa are crying. All are hugging her. They are finally relieved that she has come. Papa tells her that Bank manager called them to tell, she had come there. She tells them everything. All are sad yet happy that she is back.

Next day police comes to Kanjari's house. They question everyone. But Mayur is out. Kapil calls her. Even Bindia, Kapil's wife talks to her. Kapil tells her not to run after money or fame. Just live.

Kanjari does not say anything but feels nice. Kanjari calls Kapil for the premier party.

Mayur is with Maya in her house at Delhi. He has got a dress for her. She ask ,'what's the matter'. He says he is gifting just like that, just to celebrate their relationship.

They both are talking and drinking wine. At night Mayur reaches home to Kanjari and falls asleep. Now Sahil also stays in india at Kanjari's place only. Film finishes and Kanjari and Mayur go to Switzerland. She is seeing places in Switzerland. Goes to Salsburg, where 'Sound of Music' movie was shot. She spends good time with Mayur. She never comes to know about Maya and Mayur relationship. Mayur is living double life and keeping both the ladies happy.

Film finishes they are doing promotion. Maya also comes. She makes a speech.

Over dinner she comes to Kanjari and starts talking. Then tells her she loves Mayur. Kanjari confronts Mayur. He denys. Next day she tells this to Sahil. Sahil says he knows. Mom also knows but Mayur had told both of them not to tell Kanjari, otherwise it won't be good. Kanjari is heartbroken and tells Mayur to leave the house.

Good News of film finishing is diminished by this episode. Kanjari and Mayur are still meeting in producer's office, regarding film editing and final touches. Finally the day comes when movie is to be released. She is sitting with mom and Sahil having evening tea. Waiting for the producer's news about box office performance of the movie. Movie does well. Kanjari is relaxed. She has not slept from 2 days due to tension.

She develops fever and is taken to hospital. Doctors are unable to detect the cause of high fever. She is in delirium. Mom calls Mayur. He stays that night in the hospital. Talks to kanjari. She opens her eyes. In three days she becomes better. Mayur stays in the hospital. Life is going like this.

Mayur and Kanjari relationship has taken a grey shade. Mayur comes to see Kanjari but is staying with Maya. Everyone accepts this triangle.

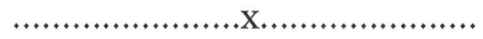

Kanjari is in hospital. Mayur is in bathroom. His mobile is on her bedside table. Suddenly a message comes on Mayur's mobile. She picks up the mobile. She is surprised to see that message as its from Sahil. It said – 'dont tell kanjari anything about Mind Game. Just contain her. She must not know about anything'. Bathroom door opens she quickly puts mobile back.

Mayur calls the nurse and tells her to give lunch to kanjari. After lunch he goes. Kanjari is left alone to tend her wounds. She is wondering what is 'mind game'. Why everyone is hiding things from her.

Even Sahil, whom she trusted blindly. Life was showing her many shades, difficult to adjust. Feeling very lonely. She did not want to tell her parent.

Both had become quiet old. They can't take so much tension. But she wonders - are they also involved?

Time is spent in hospital in thinking only. Night she sleeps poorly. Next day she has to go back home.

Papa is much happy seeing her. Mom embraces her. She is sitting on bed Mayur is sleeping next to her. He is a handsome man.

Kanjari is also not bad looking but not glamorous like Maya. But Mayur always appreciated her mind.

Next day, mom comes to her room and says she has something to tell her. She sits up attentively. Its apparent that she is not finding right words. Finally, she opens up. Mom- ' Kanjari we have much to tell you. We owe you our lives. As your father told you that when you were born we were quiet poor. We used to live in Govt. LIG flats in a DDA colony in Delhi. Papa never used to keep well because of his Asthama. I was also taking tuitions of Chemistry. But our hands were quiet tight. Had to bear responsibility of your grandparents too. Then Sahil suggested to give your mind vibration to government officials who were working on important projects. We agreed as good money was promised. We did not tell you because we felt guilty. But today I am telling you all this because you are now taking care of us in every way.

Thanks'. Kanjari does not say anything. She has nothing to say than just accept.

Mayur and Maya are in bed. Mayur lights up a cigarette and is making smoke rings. Maya is convincing Mayur that she loves him.

They both plan to abscond. He says, he will take money from Kanjari.

Mayur convinces kanjari to give him 1 cr. Mayur had taken some clothes with him, says he will be at Maya's place for a day. Kanjari keeps quiet as she does not want any tension.

Next day Iqbal Kureshi, the director had called everyone for a party on the film sets site. Iqbal takes the mike and praises Kanjari for a good story of the film and holds her responsible for all

success. He calls Kanjari on the mike. Kanjari also thanks Iqbal and producer. Then Iqbal tells everyone to enjoy. Producer opens a champaign bottle, music is playing, everyone starts dancing. Party finishes, Kanjari is looking for Mayur. Slowly all are looking for Mayur. Someone says loudly that Maya is also not there.

Kanjari's heart is sinking. She thinks why Mayur had asked her 1 cr. He had said he wants to put in some project. Party is converted into dooms project. All say they have left togather. One watchman confirms it.

They abscond. No one knows, where.

Kanjari learns from the producer that Mayur has become reasonably a big man from Kanjari's money. Mayur had put up 1 cr, taken from Kanjari, in a project and project becomes real successful. Kanjari feels rotten. She decides to confront Mayur and calls him. He does not pick his call. She leaves a message saying, 'he is an opportunistic pig'. In the meantime, Kanjari also gets her due fame in Bollywood. So, both are in Bollywood but living their separate lives. Nothing seems to happen to Mayur but Kanjari is still trying to adjust to situation.

Kanjari's film gets an award in one of Bollywood festival. Kanjari, Mayur and Iqbal all are invited by the producer and they take the award together. Kanjari is learning to keep a straight face in front of Mayur. She feels nothing for him, just plain professional joy. Mayur shys away from her. Iqbal is giving much needed support to Kanjari. They eat the dinner together. For the first time Kanjari learns that Iqbal Kureshi is a divorcee. She gets a feeling he likes her as he is telling her a lot about himself. Iqbal drops her to the hotel.

Next day she gets up late. She awakes up by Iqbal's call. He says 'did you see the newspaper today'. She say, 'No'. He says well read it I will meet you on breakfast, get ready. She calls reception and tells them to get the Newspaper. She sees the photo of her taking the award but write up is quiet scoopy. Rather than talking about her achievement they had written about triangle of Kanjari, Mayur and Maya.

She feels real anger but contains herself and waits for Iqbal. She takes bath and gets ready for him. After sometime Iqbal calls from the hotel's coffee shop for breakfast.

Iqbal tells her to confront Newspaper and put them in right place. If she does not do this, they will publish something else too.

She calls the Newspaper office. She learns, it was Mayur who gave them the information. She is in rage and both Iqbal and Kanjari get Mayur debarred from the Bollywood association. Now he can't get any work. Kanjari with help of her father gets divorce from Mayur immediately and settles for a single life.

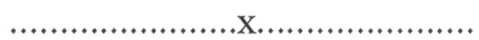

Kanjari is living now independent life with her parents. She has made some professional friends too. She is satisfied with her progress but her heart is sad after what Mayur has done. She finally accepts that Mayur is an unscrupulous kind of person. However, Kanjari is a straight kind of person but now she is learning trade techniques.

Sahil had been busy setting up medical unit in a hospital. He comes to house and discusses the newspaper issue. He is surprised by her balanced attitude.

She feels, Sahil is paying lot of attention to her. Was he showing interest in her, she wonders. One day Sahil asks her for dinner and his behavior confirms that he is interested in her. Kanjari feels uncomfortable as she always considered him as a cousin. In these things, she is still conservative. She is not able to take his interest in her nicely.

One day she is sitting in her room. Sahil comes and tells her something which tarnishes her. He says he is part of a Spiritual Think Tank which is doing lot of research in Soul matter and Vibrations. This research is sponsored by government of all countries. And all this is guided by Kanjari's mind. People in this Spiritual group have the ability to read Kanjari's mind through their 'out of body'. Kanjari objects to this research as she feels that her mind is invaded. She says she will talk to govt bodies.

Sahil says it's not possible to approach govt as this is a very confidential. But govt has issued 20 cr. for her, as her mind has helped in world's development. She is aghast hearing 20 cr. govt is giving her. Sahil further tells her that this money is in a Swiss Bank account.

Sahil takes Kanjari to Switzerland and introduces to the Swiss Bank officials. Kanjari transfers 5 cr. to her Delhi account. Kanjari is roaming Zurich with Sahil. One day he takes her to a museum. He stops in front of a picture and tells her to look at picture carefully. Well, Kanjari almost releases a small shout – 'my god this picture resembles me'. Kanjari is dumbfounded in front of the painted picture.

Sahil says that it is her picture only but from her past life, when she was a famous painter and had painted her own picture.

Kanjari is much curious now and asks him – 'how he knows'? Sahil takes her out of the museum and says, 'lets go to a restaurant'. They head for a roadside restaurant. After lunch Sahil says that he has an important news to share with her. She says, 'ok'. He says he is the only one who can see everyone's past and future life. He announces that Kanjari has a big destiny to follow if she plays all cards carefully and does not ruffle any feathers with govt officials. He further says that he has been Kanjari's spiritual guide in many lives and will continue to be. Kanjari is little scared after this revelation. She does'nt know where her life is taking her. The way Mayur went from life suddenly and Sahil's growing influence on her life, all is confusing her. That night was very troublesome for her, she was feeling little scared of Sahil. Next day she tells Sahil that she is missing her parents and wants to go back.

After coming back she meets Rakhi, her friend and tells her what Sahil told her. She also feels little apprehensive about Kanjari's life but says nothing.

When Sahil comes next day to Kanjari's house, she takes him to library and asks him how he knew Mayur before their marriage.

Sahil told her that Mayur was part of the think tank group and he is a bright guy. Sahil thought, he will be good for her but did not know that he was so much after money. Kanjari tells him further that in hospital she saw a message from him in Mayur's phone regarding Mind-game. Sahil tells her that he has got so much embroiled in the mind-game that he does not know what to do. Kanjari asks, 'what is mind-game'? Sahil replies, 'mind- game is a technique of giving your mind's vibrations to others and they work through your mind. It's called giving destiny to people. As your mind is very good, its destiny is also big which everyone is after. So I have created a kind of web of vibrations. But this game now has become so popular that I am not able to say 'no' to anyone'. Sahil further says he is trying to talk to govt officials about it.

One day suddenly Mayur calls Kanjari. She does not pick. Then he messages that he has something to tell her, which is for her benefit only. Mayur reveals that, it was Sahil who forced him to marry Kanjari. Mayur knew that he is somewhat free flowing kind of person, as opposed to Kanjari, who is a very serious in relationships. Mayur did tell this to Sahil but he said marry Kanjari. It will be good for you both professionally. Now Kanjari does not know how to rate Mayur as opoosed to Sahil. Her mind is confused. From now onwards Mayur sometimes calls Kanjari and takes from her professional tips.

They are somewhat friends. Sahil does not know this.

Sahil goes to USA for some seminar. Then only Mayur expresses desire to see her.

Kanjari calls him reluctantly after talking to her parents. Parents also don't say anything as they just want her to be happy. They know its difficult to cut completely from a person you are emotionally attached. Now Mayur has become more confident because of professional success, making him more impressive. Kanjari always found Mayur handsome and difficult to resist. Mayur is staying at their place only. When Sahil comes to know about this he shows his anger but Kanjari says, 'it's her life'. Kapil does'nt say anything as he knows Kanjari is lonely.

Slowly Mayur is becoming custodian of Kanjari's life. Professionally Kanjari is established now. Mayur is earning through Kanjari only. On the other hand, Kanjari is much tired now and want to just take life easily. But Mayur has big plans for Kanjari. One day he comes very excitedly and says he has got biggest project of his life. Kanjari is curious but when she comes to know it's a govt project, where Kanjari has to give advices she backs out. She does not want to take so much of national responsibility. Kanjari was always good in international politics and Mayur wanted to sell this ability of her's. She refuses but Mayur cajoles her, says, it is a big opportunity to become world famous. Kanjari has no power to refuse him, against his charms. Sahil is absent from her life as he has been given a teaching assignment in USA.

Well, the real reason for Mayur to propose this was his diminishing savings. Maya was having an affair with some producer and thus he was out of her life for the time being. In absence of any real life support, Kanjari had just given herself to Mayur.

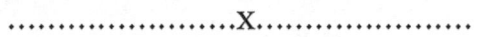

When Sahil comes back he shows displeasure to this arrangement between Mayur and Kanjari. But Kanjari says she is kind of happy and has accepted Mayur as he is. Govt is also happy with Mayur as he is ready to use Kanjari's mind for larger good, whereas Sahil is little conservative on this matter. Mayur is now moving in big govt lobbies and often his name surfaces in newspaper headlines. Whereas Sahil settles for less fame and is occupied with his medical project. He is living with his friend. Life has taken 360 degree turn for Mayur, making him little pompous.

Kanjari remains as an anchoring figure in both men's life.

There is a big construction project coming in one of the interior states of India. Kanjari has been introduced by Mayur as the marketing consultant in this project.

Kanjari is an idea person, more of an academic professional and not so knowledgeable on the practical aspect of the construction game. She has given big ideas on tourism for that state but does not know that mafia is quiet rampant in this part of the country. Infact some govt officials also have mafia background. Mayur tells nothing to Kanjari and gets all loans approved by the govt.

Kanjari has put lot of effort in chalking out marketing and communication strategies for the project. But project gets stopped because of local elections. On Mayur request she also takes part in that state election. Mayur makes this election his major PR project- meeting all official of the state, businessmen and general public. People come to know they are involved in the development of their state. Kanjari also thinks this is a major progress. After elections the local govt and even all business contacts seem to be enjoying a siesta. All seem to be relaxing as now elections are over.

Kanjari accepts this is the pace of work here in this interior state. Mayur tells her to have patience.

Well it is now one year after the election but no one has called Kanjari and Mayur for the work. She asks Mayur but he evades the answer. He himself does'nt know the answer. Kanjari being a hard task master sends Mayur to the state to find out the reason of this delay. In a week Mayur comes back. He is in depressed state. After long grilling Mayur answers Kanjari. Actually he is feeling scared of Kanjari. He reveals that everything is in doldrums in that interior state. No one seems to take the responsibility. Govt officials said that they have given the loan money to the construction company but they have not started the work.

Construction company refuses to meet Mayur, saying funds are not enough. Mayur does not know whom to blame. Kanjari feels he is hiding something. She calls Sahil and tells him to talk to Mayur as Mayur looks very worried.

Sahil and Mayur spend one hour in the library then Sahil calls Kanjari. Mayur is sitting with his face in his hands. Sahil presides over – 'Kanjari there is a big time problem here'. Kanjari panics, says –'what happened', is Mayur all right?' Sahil- 'no he is not all right' neither we are. You both have been called for an enquiry by the Central Govt on that Construction Project.

Looks people have siphoned that loan money. They want to ask you two because you are the authority on that project. Kanjari just sinks on the sofa.

She looks at Mayur who is just sitting without any word.

Kanjari finally asks Sahil-' what to do now Sahil, how to get away from this enquiry'.

Sahil reply's – 'well don't try to run away from the enquiry. Face the govt. Only saving grace is your reputation.

They might not like to argue with you because of your name'. Its dawning on Kanjari that Mayur has put her in a big trouble. Sahil says he will ask his lawyer to be there and he will also be there. Enquiry is next week. For next four days lawyer comes and makes an explanation to be presented in front of the enquiry. Kanjari also visits her colony temple with mom and prays to all gods for help. Kanjari is thinking that whatever work she takes, she gets into trouble. First it was the film and now this consultancy. She does not understand why people don't take her seriously despite her credentials.

Other side of the story which Sahil and Mayur want to hide from Kanjari is that people are troubling her in this state not only because of money but also because they want Kanjari's destiny i.e her mind. Sahil does not want this to be discussed openly and prepares the argument to be put in front of Central Govt accordingly.

The day of the enquiry comes. Kanjari goes with her lawyer, Mayur and Sahil. She is feeling apprehensive but confident.

Central Govt puts a complain that work has not started and the required parties are not replying and don't want to give back the assigned money too. Kanjari's lawyer starts his argument and says that Kanjari and Mayur are only 'idea people' and quality controllers. Infact loan was disbursed to the construction party by the local govt officials. Hence local govt officials should be responsible.

Actually Central Govt is well aware of the poor status of local govt official and knows only Kanjari is capable of getting the work finished. That's why they have put the enquiry to Kanjari and Mayur.

Kanjari's lawyer further tells the authorities that in the state where the project is situated, mafia is rampant in construction business. So they should put up a local enquiry and once the issue of the money is solved they should contact Kanjari to start the work. Kanjari comes back in a good mood because authorities agree to lawyer's argument. After few days she comes to know that Central Authorities have assigned the local IPS officer to talk to the construction company. In two months whole thing is solved and Kanjari is given an invitation letter to come. Kanjari's lawyer sends a reply to that letter. Kanjari is doing all communication through a lawyer because she does not want to take any chance. Mayur is also happy as his future depends on this project. It was decided earlier only that Mayur will get the major share of the fees which Kanjari will get from this project, so he is quiet attentive to the job now.

Marketing work starts after six months and Kanjari takes help of all Delhi based marketing and advertising companies as that state is not so developed. Projects finishes and the tourist spot is inaugurated by the PM with much fan and fare. The successful completion of this project put another feather in Kanjari's portfolio i.e of being a Marketing and Communication Consultant.

Sahil also comes in the inauguration, meets the PM and tells him that the issue of destiny is solved as this state now has a destiny of tourism. However, Sahil does not tell anything to Kanjari about this conversation with PM.

Kanjari's destiny has finally opened and she is getting lots of requests from govt. Mayur is also happy that he is getting so many opportunities to make money but Sahil is not happy with this work pace. He warns Kanjari to go slow.

Kanjari takes his advice and is waiting for a project of her choice.

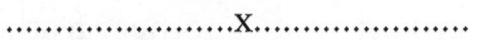

One day Kanjari is sitting with Sahil and mom in the drawing room. Mayur enters the house and announces to Kanjari that they have to leave in 2 days to Russia. Kanjari is speechless. Sahil rolls his eyes and asks – 'why, why she has to go to Russia?'. Mayur- ' I have promised the Russian government that Kanjari will guide them on a international business project and will help Russia to rebuilt itself.' Sahil -' I hope you don't do any other fiasco. I will also come.'

They all board the plane for Russia.

In Russia, they are welcomed by the foreign minister and are taken to a govt guest house. They are introduced to a manager kind of person, who speaks English. Kanjari and all go to bed early as they have to meet the foreign minister at 10 sharp in a office which is on the other side of the quarter. Kanjari had said that she will only work for the first half of the day, as mom would be alone in the quarter.

In the meeting, foreign minister explains the problems on which he needed guidance. It takes one week for Kanjari to read every document and chalk out a plan. She heavily does internet research. Project is about making Russia's foreign trade robust. She creates a business brief for the Russian economists who would be working on the project. Two of the economists who speak English are called for reading the brief. Once they are comfortable with the brief, they are told that in a week's time they would be required to present a paper which will explain in detail the exportable item from Russia. In this one week, Kanjari and others roam Russia. Final day comes when the paper has to be presented by the economists. All comes to an end satisfactorily. Kanjari, Mayur and Sahil get their monetary due. Kanjari also gives some money to mom as she had been a quiet companion to her in this effort. In this project Kanjari was given the status of Special Consultant. This is how she makes a mark in foreign affairs also.

When they reach India, its just one day before Holi festival. Everyone is in Holi mood. Mom does Pooja and everyone apply Gulal (dry color) on eachother. Suddenly bell rings and Maya arrives with her producer friend. She comes running to Mayur and hugs him. Mayur is looking much happy. Kanjari is aghast, Sahil is looking angry. Mayur says – ' This is a Holi surprise. I had called Maya as she has been wanting to meet me for months'. Maya does'nt say anything, just greets Maya. They take lunch and after that all settle down in the drawing room. Maya and Mayur are talking on the side sofa. Kanjari can't hear anything. After sometime Mayur announces that Maya and him have another plan for a film, which Kanjari has to write. Neither Kanjari nor Sahil like Mayur's this high-handed attitude.

Sahil approaches Mayur and says – 'did you take Kanjari's permission before talking to Maya about the next film.' Mayur – 'No its between me and Kanjari, you don't interfare'. Sahil-' how I don't interfare, she is just back from Russia. You are just using her for your monetary gain. Give her some rest'.

Mayur – 'Well she has all life to rest. Now Maya's producer friend is interested in making a movie with Kanjari. He might be busy later on or will take someone else.' Sahil – ' Well just now Kanjari can't write anything. We will see later'. Saying this Sahil tells

Maya and her friend to go. Mayur is visibly upset. Sahil and Mayur are arguing. Kanjari tells Mayur she is sleeping in Mom's room and goes.

Next morning Kanjari finds Mayur fast asleep when she gets up. She gets ready and tries to wake up Mayur for breakfast. But he says he well eat later, he is tired. Kanjari, Sahil and Mom take breakfast. Sahil is looking quiet satisfied but Kanjari is worried for Mayur as she is in love with him.

Kanjari spends whole day roaming in the corridor. Mayur has developed slight fever. She makes soup for Mayur and gives him in bed. He is not talking to her. She gives him a shoulder hug and remains quiet.

Mayur sleeps whole day.

Next day is Mayur's birthday. No one remembers. Kanjari puts a rose on his bedside table and puts a 'happy birthday' note. Mayur is little better seeing the rose. Kanjari tells him that she has booked a table for two in Hyatt for dinner. Mayur and Kanjari take a quiet dinner in Hyatt that evening and decide not to talk work at all. They laugh on their fight and Kanjari makes up with Mayur. At night they spend long hours listening to music and fall asleep in each other arms.

................x................

Sahil is watching Kanjari and Mayur's relationship closely. At times Kanjari feels he is

jealous but he is quiet concerned. One day when Mayur is not there, he catches

Kanjari and convinces her to talk to him. He warns her against Mayur. He says- 'Kanjari don't let Mayur rule your life. He is not a very right guy'. Kanjari- 'Why what happened ?, you don't like us both.' Sahil – 'No Kanjari, its not like that. He has taken up another research project of the Spiritual Group which he has said, he will do from your mind.' Kanjari says- what research? Sahil – 'Well he has taken a research on the Soul matter, to be done by you.' Kanjari- Why you did not tell me? Sahil- 'because he told me not to tell you.' Kanjari – 'ok I will ask him'.

Kanjari confronts Mayur, the moment he comes back. Mayur tells her about 'Soul Keeping', where some yogis give shelter to roaming souls. And they do research on these souls to understand their origin. Kanjari finds it interesting and decides to join this group. Sahil also agrees to help them and becomes the leader. He starts the meditation the next day which goes on for one hour and tells Kanjari also to sit with closed eyes. It takes two days for Kanjari to gain some stability in meditation.

After a week she is sitting for meditation and goes deep. She goes into trance and suddenly panics and opens her eyes. She gets a jolt as she opens her eyes suddenly from a deep meditation. In the trance she was roaming in the sky and looking at earth from up. She tells this to Sahil.

He expresses joy but Kanjari is scared, so he tells her to stop. But Mayur is persistent that this project has to be done. Sahil cancels the research, much to Kajari's comfort.

However Mayur is not happy atall.

Kanjari takes an oath to keep her self away from all spiritual practices and be in materialistic world.

..................x................

Phase - II

Kanjari

Kanjari is fifty years now. She is living her life with Mayur, Sahil, Kapil and Kapil's family. Mom has passed away, Kapil has shifted his base to Delhi only. He is doing his private Computer Programming which is going ok. He is also 40 years now and wants to take life little easy. Kanjari is helping him monetarily also. He has got a 10 year old boy, who is quiet pampered by Kanjari. Sahil is busy in his medical project. Mayur is slowly diminishing himself in alcohol as he has nothing to do. Kanjari keeps herself busy in the house with Bindia Bhabhi and looks after her investments. Kanjari is becoming quiet a financial wizard.

Kanjari is much worried about Mayur. After mom's death they dissolved their divorce and did a court marriage.

Mayur told her that he will look after her. Sahil also has become much soft towards Kanjari, as she has rescued him many times from the monetary tight spots. Mayur also is dependent on Kanjari as his savings have diminished.

Kanjari is looking for some consultancy but she is not getting it. Kanjari sees another dream of Saraswati where Saraswati is putting a halo crown on Kanjari's head and whispers in ears - 'look inside and search for the true path'.

She ponders a lot about this dream and tells Sahil about it.

She tells Sahil to revive that Soul Researching project which they had cancelled. She tells Sahil to complete it without her involvement, except her mind.

However, she gives a thematic guidance that with soul preservation, he can also upgrade the soul intelligence, when souls sleep after the body dies. This research becomes the research of the year. Whole world hails Kanjari. Sahil, Mayur and Kapil all are happy. Spiritual Community decides to keep a function in honour of Kanjari and deems her to be Saraswati. She is awarded a shield, Saraswati written over it.

Though Kanjari is respected in the spiritual community, govt has not given her much recognition. And real recognition according to her is to leave her mind totally and stop using it for various projects. Kanjari talks about it to Sahil. He is much confident of her position after getting the Saraswati shield. Kanjari advises him to approach UN for this issue as

Kanjari's mind has been involved in World's project. Sahil on Kanjari's behalf writes to UN and gets an affirmative answer. Now all govt bodies of all nations have been informed by the UN that Kanjari's mind cannot be involved without her permission.

............................x......................

Kanjari is now satisfied that she has been recognised. Three months have passed after the UN decision. One day Sahil comes looking very worried. She is sitting with Mayur and asks, 'what's the matter?'. Sahil reveals that all world govt have complained to Indian govt that after closing entries of 'out of bodies' of different officials, in

Kanjari's mind, things have become quiet difficult. Mayur panics and says why don't we take off this rule to not enter Kanjari's mind but Sahil has strong resolve to solve the problem differently. He says, 'I will change the vibration mode, this will solve the problem to quiet an extent'. Sahil writes to UN and Indian Govt about this and things start becoming normal slowly.

Kanjari is looking after everyone at home and everyone is happy with her except Mayur, who still wants Kanjari's mind to be sold. Kanjari is slowly getting tired of Mayur as he just wants to drink and expect Kanjari to keep him happy. Mayur's all promises that he will look after Kanjari are falling flat.

She depends much on Kapil and Sahil for emotional support. On the other side, Maya's affair with the producer is also finished and she is living a single life. Mayur is in contact with her. As usual she has accepted this situation. Now she works with Sahil on the Soul Preservation account. She gives thematic guidance and Sahil preserves the souls. Mayur is jealous of their relationship. Kanjari has lot of respect for Sahil for his talent.

After successful completion of Soul Preservation project Kanjari wants to do something which she always wanted to do i.e International Politics. Kanjari is not a storehouse on facts but has a very analytical mind. She has unique solutions to the world problems. She has made many notes on the topic but tells no one. Mayur asks, 'what she is working on'. She just ignores him.

She does not consider him worthy of telling such complex topic.' She calls Sahil and says she has solution to many world's and domestic political problems. Sahil is impressed, Kanjari just tells him some problems and says, 'she will tell the govt only, as solutions are highly confidential'.

Kanjari is a perfect diplomat which reflects in her personal as well as professional life both.

Kanjari takes up many domestic and international issues and gives a thematic solution. Issues are relations with Pakistan, China and India's rightful place in the Asian sub-continent. She gives a unique solution to Pakistan relation and Kashmir. She also touches Cricket world and comes up with new ideas.

Internationally she takes up FDI issue and writes also on World Education.

Sahil creates a Facebook page of Kanjari and slowly her status gets raised to an International Speaker. She is called by many Universities to speak on various topics. A novelist approaches her to write her life story and book is released with much fanfare. She gets a world mapping.

Kanjari strongly feels for Tibet where she praises Dalai Lama, on which China press writes hot reviews. It gets covered on Indian TV channels too. Her favourite country is Bhutan which came out with the concept of 'Gross National Happiness'. She also writes about 10 Happiest Countries of the World, as a column in Times of India.

Well, this fame of her's does not go right with Mayur. He is much jealous and keeps snapping on her. Mayur does not have a very mature knowledge about world affairs. He is more of a Bollywood person.

Kanjari ignores it and keeps herself busy with other members of the house. Mayur's charisma is dissolving, Kanjari is no more bothered about Mayur. He is just living in the house without much interaction with her.

This infuriates Mayur as he always considered Kanjari his property and tried his physical charm over her but it's no more working. Mayur's gold fitch is going from his hand which is making him much insecure. One day they both have a fight and Mayur takes out a gun in rage and shoots her. She is injured and hospitalised. Mayur goes in police custody.

However Sahil is against sending him in custody but Kapil puts his foot down and does not listen to anyone.

This is how finally Mayur's relationship ends with Kanjari.

Kanjari is now dependent on Kapil and his family for emotional support. Sahil is busy in work. Kanjari is recuperating and has become quiet philosophical. She joins Art of Living and spends much time with this community. On the other side Mayur contacts Maya from jail and requests her to help. He comes out on bail and Maya with her contacts manages that this news does'nt surface in press. Mayur shifts to Mumbai, of which Kanjari has no clue. Govt is very concerned about this attack on Kanjari and orders a thorough investigation in the Mayur case. After sometime Police comes to Kanjari's house and tells her that Mayur only had planned the kidnapping of Kanjari, which had happened years back. They tell her confidentially that Sahil also was involved. Kanjari is shocked. Police takes Sahil and Mayur both in custody. Kapil is also shaken with this news.

Sahil and Mayur become friends in jail and are doing their spiritual business. Sahil gave vibrations of Kanjari to many inmates. Sahil is ready to use Kanjari's mind which Mayur also wants. They use Kanjari's mind and do jail authorities work of making reports, in-mates admission etc. They both are quiet fast and thorough. Jail authorities are quiet happy with them. They finally get the bail on their good behaviour. Police can't do anything as Mayur and Sahil manage to hire a very good lawyer with the help of jail authorities.

Sahil and Mayur are in Delhi only but Kanjari does'nt know. Sahil with his contacts is doing his consultancy work with

Kanjari's mind. He is becoming quiet popular in govt circles. Kanjari is living a reclusive life, involved with Art of Living. One day Iqbal Kureshi, who likes Kanjari calls her and tells that Sahil is out and probably using her mind as he is doing lot of work. She goes with him to meet Sahil, who now is current govt's consultant and sits in north block. Kanjari confronts him and says, 'why are you using my mind'.

Sahil does not hide, takes Kanjari in confidence and tells his much hidden secret that he is an Intelligence Officer, infact head of all intelligence agencies of the world. He accepts that he has been using her mind since very young and created the vibration web to reach everyone's mind. This is an espionage work.

It finally dawns on Kanjari that she has to live in this situation and make best for her. Kanjari says, 'kindly close everyone's entry to my mind and I will help you in intelligence work'. She learns meditation from Sahil and start using her third eye. Third eye can show her the past and future. She is guided by third eye as Sahil tells her.

But she is not so convinced by this technique as she believes that humans can change their destiny by their own effort. She takes third eye as just a guiding tool but not as the final answer. Sahil is not so convinced but does not say anything.

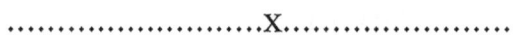

Kanjari is working for Intelligence Agencies in full swinge.

Sahil is also with her. Mayur has gone to Mumbai with Maya and kanjari is not on talking terms with him. Kanjari has resigned to the fact that she has to cooperate with the govt and with the world at large. She is working for the NATO's Peace Programme, consulting as to how integrate the migrating population of war ridden countries. She becomes an international figure as she presents her paper in international headquarters of NATO in Brussels.

She is resting in hotel in Brussels and Mayur comes to meet her. She is alone in the room, she gets scared.

After repeated calling she opens the door and lets Mayur in as he says, 'he has to tell a very important thing'.

Mayur comes, takes a seat in her room and says, 'no need to be scared', I never wanted to harm you. I did not know that pistol was loaded that night.' First Kanjari does not believe. He further says, he kidnapped her because Sahil told him to do as both were in debt and needed to pay off the parties. He says,' I am loose character but I respect you a lot and can never think of harming you.'

Kanjari does'nt know whether to believe him or not. He says he can help her regain her mind. Kanjari asks, 'how'? He says, 'he wants her to meet jail authorities'. Kanjari agrees. Kanjari and Mayur come back to Delhi. Mayur is staying at his place. Kanjari tells everything to Kapil. He also agrees to meet jail authorities. Jail authorities tell kanjari that one day in jail Sahil called USA and just two days after, his and Mayur's bail request comes from a lawyer. Jail authorities said he never told who he called in USA. Mayur also did not know.

Mayur is living with Maya but is still emotionally attached to Kanjari. Kanjari has gotten over Mayur but not Mayur, as his relationship with Maya is more of sexual in nature. Mayur meets Kanjari on weekends as on other days she does her consultancy with creative agencies. Mayur is

looking after Kanjari as he realizes his mistakes. Kapil also has come to know reality about Sahil.

What Kanjari does not know is that Sahil only had sent Mayur to tell her everything. So that he gains confidence of Kanjari as Sahil does not want to take her responsibility alone. Sahil has asked Mayur to maintain friendly relations with Kanjari. All this is because

Kanjari's mind is key to their life.

After knowing about Sahil, Kanjari is feeling insecure. She is sick with anxiety. She takes emotional support of Kapil. Kapil also has no solution.

Only respite in Kanjari's life is her work.

She is feeling sick with anxiety. She meets Rakhi and discusses about Sahil and Mayur. Rakhi advises her to go to police but Kanjari is not so sure. She tries to gain support on her Facebook page, that her mind should be freed. She also tries to gain support in creative industry i.e Bollywood. Kanjari has a following on twitter too. Even Spiritual group has extended their support to her. Kanjari does not know how to fight with Sahil, who is like a resident evil. Kanjari is trying to win her case with dialogue with different groups and creating a public opinion. Sahil and Mayur also agree to free Kanjari.

This is how she slowly wins the heart of her country people and they hail her as 'Saraswati' – the Indian Goddess of Knowledge.

..........................x......................

www.ingramcontent.com/pod-product-compliance
Lightning Source LLC
LaVergne TN
LVHW041853070526
838199LV00045BB/1570